# *The*
# TWO BEST FRIENDS

*Story and Pictures*

*by*

*Elizabeth Koda-Callan*

WORKMAN PUBLISHING, NEW YORK

Library of Congress Cataloging-in-Publication Data

Koda-Callan, Elizabeth.
The two best friends / by Elizabeth Koda-Callan.
p.   cm.
Summary: A lonely little girl who has just moved to a new neighborhood finds a dog and strikes up a friendship with the girl next door.
ISBN 1-56305-730-1
[1. Dogs — Fiction.  2. Friendship—Fiction.  3. Moving, Household—Fiction.  4. Chicken pox—Fiction.]  I. Title
PZ7. K8175Tw   1994
[E]—dc20                                                          94-25767
                                                                         CIP
                                                                          AC

Workman books are available at special discounts when purchased in bulk for premiums and sales promotions, as well as for fundraising or educational use. Special editions or book excerpts can also be created to specification. For details, contact the Special Sales Director at the address below.

Workman Publishing Company, Inc.
708 Broadway
New York, NY 10003
Printed in Hong Kong
First printing October 1994
10 9 8 7 6 5 4 3 2 1

*For Carol Bresnay*
*and*
*Zippy, Ginger, and Chelsea*

$O$nce there was a little girl who
was shy and a bit lonely. She had just
moved into a new neighborhood with her
parents. And she longed for a good friend.

I hate moving," she thought, as she looked sadly out the kitchen window in her new home. Her mother was busy unpacking boxes.

"Isn't that a great big backyard?" said her mother. "That maple tree would be perfect for a swing."

"I guess," said the little girl. She sighed. "I miss my friends."

"I saw a playground down the street," said her mother. "Why don't you go for a walk and look around?"

The little girl didn't feel at all like going for a walk. But she went out anyway.

Yes, there was a playground at the end of the street. The little girl sat down on one of the empty swings. "What good is a playground," she thought, "without a friend?"

Before long she noticed a dog wandering around the playground. "It looks as if he could use a friend, too," she thought, as she absentmindedly picked up a stick and tossed it in his direction. The dog ran for the stick and happily brought it back to her. "Thanks, dog," she said, as she patted his head. "I guess you can be my friend this afternoon."

The dog had a golden coat, wavy ears, and a feathery tail. Around his neck, he wore a red collar. He was the most beautiful dog the little girl had ever seen.

After they played awhile, the little girl patted him and said, "It's time for you to go home."

She was feeling better as she started for her own home—playing with the dog had cheered her. She was partway home when she realized he was following her. She stopped. He stopped, too. "You should be going home," she scolded gently. But the dog wagged his feathery tail and followed her to her front door.

When her father came home that evening, he said, "There's a dog sitting on the front steps. He looks a lot like a retriever."

"What's a retriever?" asked the little girl.

"It's a dog who likes to go after things and bring them back," her father replied.

The little girl ran to the window. "He followed me home from the playground. It looks as if he still wants to play," she said to her parents.

The little girl was worried. "It's getting dark out," she said, "and the dog must be hungry."

Her mother and father looked at each other for a few moments. Then her father said, "Okay, bring him in and we'll feed him. But just for tonight."

"The dog has a collar, so he must belong to someone," said her mother.

The little girl nodded. "I understand," she said. "Meanwhile, I'm going to call him Murphy."

The next day the little girl's father put an ad in the newspaper and tacked up signs describing the lost dog.

Murphy seemed quite content where he was. He and the little girl now played together every day after school. He especially liked fetching an old tennis ball. He enjoyed this game so much that he began bringing her all sorts of things.

He brought her a sock from the
laundry pile in the basement.

He brought her a wooden spoon
that her mother left on the table.

He picked up her old bicycle horn
from the garage and brought it, honking,

into the house. He even found a straw hat
she had misplaced.

One day the little girl and Murphy were playing in the backyard. He ran toward her with something in his mouth and laid it at her feet. It was a small stuffed toy.

"Where did you get this?" she asked him, as she picked up the toy. Then she saw the hole in the hedge that separated her house from the neighbor's.

"Oh, Murphy," she said, "we have to return this."

At that moment, a dark-haired girl ran into the yard.

"Are you looking for this?" The little girl held up the stuffed toy.

"Yes, it's mine," said the girl. "I live next door. My name is Katie."

"I was just coming to return it," said the little girl. "This is Murphy. I'm sorry he took it. He loves to fetch things."

"I saw him wiggling under the hedge," said Katie. "You're so lucky to have a dog. I can't have one. My mother is allergic to dogs." Then she said shyly, "Do you mind if I play with you and Murphy for a while?"

"Oh, that would be great," said the little girl.

The girls played all afternoon with Murphy.

The next day they went together to the playground. The little girl was delighted to have someone her own age to play with.

When the telephone rang that evening, the little girl heard her mother say, "Yes, I'll let you know. Thank you for calling."

"That was Murphy's owners. They read the ad in the paper," her mother told her. The little girl held her breath.

"What about Murphy?"

"Next week, his owners are moving to an apartment that doesn't allow pets," said her mother, "so they can't take Murphy with them. They asked if we'd like to keep him."

"Oh, can we? Please?" the little girl asked.

Her mother nodded.

"Hooray!" shouted the little girl. "Murphy's here to stay." She could hardly wait to tell Katie the good news.

But when morning came, something was wrong. The little girl's face was flushed, and her forehead was hot. Red splotches were beginning to appear on her neck and cheeks.

"I'm afraid you have chicken pox," her mother told her gently. "You must go back to bed."

"But I want to see Katie," cried the little girl.

"First you must get better," her mother told her. "Chicken pox is catching. It will be at least a week before you can have visitors."

The days went by very slowly. The little girl felt lonely and bored. Then one morning, Murphy came in dragging her long red scarf behind him like a woolly snake. It gave her an idea.

The little girl got paper and crayons and drew a picture of herself dotted with chicken pox. She put the picture in an envelope and told Murphy to carry it next door to Katie.

When Katie received it, she laughed at the picture, made a drawing of herself, and wrote, "I miss you. Get better soon."

Murphy took Katie's envelope back to the little girl. Then she took a new piece of paper and made a squiggle on it for Katie to complete as her own picture. Soon Murphy was back with a drawing of a big green dragon with the squiggly line as its long, spiked tail.

It was a lively game. The days
passed more quickly as Murphy ran

back and forth eagerly with pictures and
messages.

Soon the little girl was well enough to have visitors. Katie ran over at once to see her friend. And right behind her came Murphy, with something in his mouth.

"What's he carrying?" asked the little girl.

"Something special for you," said Katie. The little girl took the box that Murphy was carrying—a small box topped with a blue satin bow. Carefully she opened it. There, lying on soft cotton, was a tiny golden puppy on a gold chain.

"A puppy charm necklace. What a beautiful get-well gift," said the little girl.

"It's more than that," said Katie. "It's to thank you for sharing Murphy and for being such a good friend."

The little girl smiled at Katie and hugged her. "I thought it would take a long time to make a friend," she said. "Now I have *two* best friends."

And she gave Murphy a hug, too. For she knew it takes a special kind of retriever to fetch a friend.

# About the Author

Elizabeth Koda-Callan is a designer, illustrator, and best-selling children's book author who lives in New York City. She grew up in Connecticut with Zippy, a black lab who was a constant companion and true friend.

She is the creator of the Magic Charm book series, which includes THE MAGIC LOCKET, THE SILVER SLIPPERS, THE GOOD LUCK PONY, THE TINY ANGEL, THE SHINY SKATES, and THE CAT NEXT DOOR.